"BECAUSE You ARE ALIVE, EVERYTHING IS POSSIBLE."
— Thich NHAT Hanh

THIS BOOK IS DEDICATED TO YOU, WONDERFUL You!

_____

YOUR NAME

www.enchantedlion.com

First Edition, published in 2018 by Enchanted Lion Books
67 West Street, 317A, Brooklyn, NY 11222
Text and illustrations Copyright © 2018 by Ohara Hale
Design and handlettering: Ohara Hale

A CIP record is on file with the Library of Congress
ISBN 978-1-59270-257-2
Printed in China by R.R. Donnelley Asia Printing Solutions

First Printing
1 3 5 7 9 8 6 4 2

BE STILL,
life

ENCHANTED LION BOOKS
NEW YORK

BE STILL, *life*, BE STILL
LIKE THE SURFACE OF A POND
AND YOU'LL SEE THE FISH
SWIM THROUGH
THE CLOUDS and THE FRONDS!

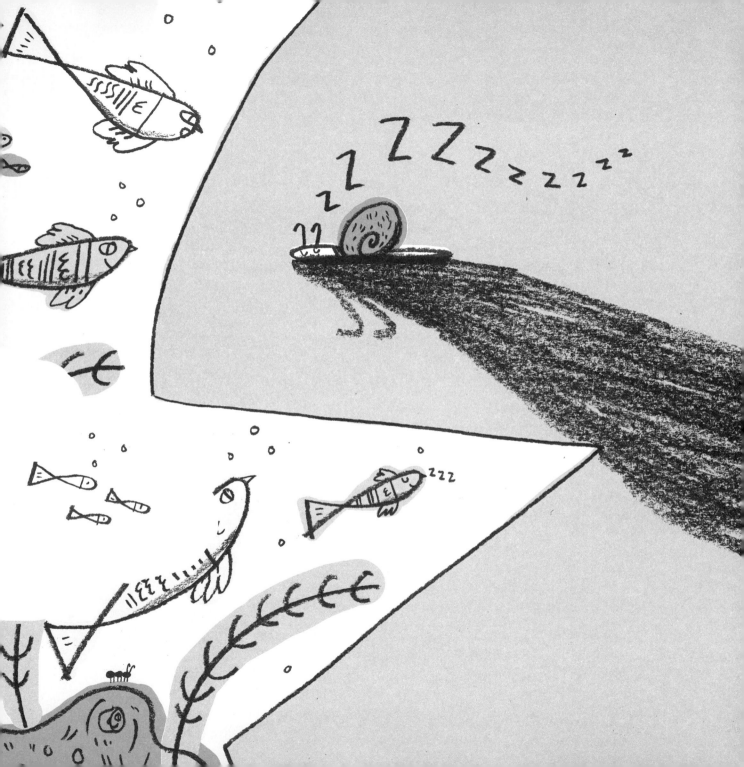

hello

NOW LET US LOOK UP AT THE LEAVES IN THE TREES.
DO YOU SEE HOW THEY SWAY IN THE WHISPERING BREEZE?

CAN YOU HEAR EACH LEAF MOVE?
CAN YOU HEAR THOSE BREAKING FREE?

AND WHAT ABOUT THE SKY STRETCHING OUT BEYOND THOSE LEAVES?
IF THE SKY HAD A SONG, WHAT DO YOU THINK IT WOULD SING?

BE STILL, *life*, BE STILL
LIKE FRUIT IN A BOWL.

AND YOU MIGHT HEAR THE HUM
OF A CRISP SUMMER'S APPLE,
OR A PEAR JOINING IN WITH A
PEAR KIND OF BABBLE!

IT'S TRUE THAT BANANAS
SING VERY WELL TOO.
SWEET SONGS OF YELLOW,
ORANGE, PINK, AND EVEN BLUE!

SHHHHHHHHH, *life*, BE STILL,
AS QUIET AS A MOUSE...
AND YOU MIGHT HEAR THE
TAPPING OF TINY MICE FEET
DANCING THROUGH THE HOUSE
AND INTO THE STREET.

HOW ABOUT THIS, CAN YOU HEAR
NOTHING TOO?
IN THE SILENCE AND THE STILLNESS
THERE IS SOMETHING - IS IT YOU?

BE STILL, life, BE STILL
AT THE BREAK OF DAWN,
AND YOU'LL FEEL THE SUN'S LIGHT
WHEN YOU HEAR THE MORNING'S SONG.

NOW WHAT DO YOU SMELL IF YOU
STOP AND TAKE A WHIFF?

CAN YOU SMELL THIS BOOK'S PAGES,
OR THE SCENT OF DOG LIPS?

'DOG LIPS?!

FOR IT TAKES THOUSANDS OF FLOWERS,
HUNDREDS EACH HOUR,
TO MAKE ONE GOLDEN SPOONFUL
OF SWEET HONEYBEE POWER!

NOW LET'S TAKE A MINUTE AND IMAGINE SITTING IN THE GRASS. AT FIRST YOU SEE GREEN UNTIL YOU NOTICE AN ANT. THERE'S ONE, THEN TWO, THREE AND THEN FOUR. SUDDENLY YOU REALIZE THERE ARE SO MANY MORE!

YOU SPOT A LADYBUG, A SLUG,
AND THE FLUTTERING BUTTERFLIES.
YOU SEE BIRDS UP ABOVE
AND HEAR THEIR SONG IN THE SKY.

You feel the sun on your face
and smell the blossoming flowers.
You are peaceful and calm here—
for a moment or for hours.

YOU CAN GO TO THIS PLACE
ANYTIME THAT YOU'D LIKE.
YOU JUST HAVE TO
BE STILL, *life* (THATS YOU!),
AND YOU'LL FIND IT INSIDE.

SO REMEMBER TO GO SLOW,
LIKE THE SNAIL AND TURTLE TOO.
FOR WHEN YOU DO YOU WILL SEE
THAT **EVERYTHING** IS
STILL and MOVING,
          JUST LIKE YOU!